The Magic Party

Blackie Bears

Ginger's Nine Lives Pamela Oldfield
The Friday Parcel Ann Pilling
The Monster in the Cupboard Jacqueline Wilson
James and the TV Star Michael Hardcastle
Monkey Business Mark Burgess
The Tall Story of Wilbur Small Martin Waddell
Green Gloves Angela Bull
Flyaway Frankie Chris Powling
Class Three and the Beanstalk Martin Waddell
Wayne's Wedding John Escott
Bella's Dragon Chris Powling
The Magic Party Michael Hardcastle
The Jungle Sale Ann Pilling
Wayne's Luck John Escott
The Party in the Lift Jacqueline Wilson
Lucky Thunder Mark Burgess
Joanna's Goal Michael Hardcastle
Pink Socks Angela Bull
A Shaggy Dog Story Pamela Oldfield
Lost Property Terrance Dicks
Butterfingers Chris Powling
James and the House of Fun Michael Hardcastle
George and the Dragon Terrance Dicks
Something Old, Something New John Escott
Tim the Trumpet Elisabeth Beresford
Batman and Other Animals Linda Jennings
Wesley at the Water Park Chris Powling
Steaming Sam Terrance Dicks
Luke's Dog Linda Jennings
Marlene the Monster Tessa Krailing
The Cat With No Name Pamela Oldfield
Jamie and the Rola Polar Bear Elisabeth Beresford

The Magic Party

Michael Hardcastle

Illustrated by
Vanessa Julian-Ottie

A Blackie Bear

BLACKIE CHILDREN'S BOOKS

Published by the Penguin Group
Penguin Books Ltd, 27 Wrights Lane, London W8 5TZ, England
Penguin Books USA Inc., 375 Hudson Street, New York, New York 10014, USA
Penguin Books Australia Ltd, Ringwood, Victoria, Australia
Penguin Books Canada Ltd, 10 Alcorn Avenue, Toronto, Ontario, Canada M4V 3B2
Penguin Books (NZ) Ltd, 182-190 Wairau Road, Auckland 10, New Zealand

Penguin Books Ltd, Registered Offices: Harmondsworth, Middlesex, England

First published 1988 by Blackie Children's Books

1 3 5 7 9 10 8 6 4 2

Made and printed in Great Britain by Butler & Tanner Ltd, Frome and London

A CIP catalogue record for this book is available from the British Library

ISBN 0 216 921082

About the Author

Michael Hardcastle is one of Britain's best known children's authors. He has published more than ninety books on all sorts of subjects, though he is probably best known for his sports novels, notably football, horse riding, netball and motocross. He writes for a wide age range, from 6-year-olds to teenagers and makes regular visits to schools, libraries and book fairs to talk to children and find out what they want to read. His books for Blackie include *Double Holiday, Snookered!* and *James and the TV Star,* a Blackie Bear.

'Listen Lisa,' said Katie eagerly, 'I've got something terrific to tell you. To tell everybody.'

'Tell me first,' said Lisa. 'After all, I am your best friend.'

But Katie wanted to tell everyone at once. She led the way across the playground to the corner by the old bakery where all secrets were swapped.

'Jessica—Sharmilla—Bobby! Come over here, quick!' she called loudly. 'I've something very special to tell you all.'

Then she spotted Melanie, who seemed to be heading for the same part of the playground. 'Mel! Come and listen to this.'

Melanie just waved a hand to show she'd heard. She was holding a package in her other hand and chattering away to Ross and Belinda. Just behind them was Simon, trying to catch everything that was said. Simon hated to miss out on anything.

'Oh, come on, Katie, don't

keep us waiting!' Jessica pleaded, putting her hands together as if she were praying. 'I hate having to wait for anything.'

'You'll know in a moment, Jess,' Katie promised with a smile.

'Is it to do with school, what you're going to tell us, Katie?' Sharmilla wanted to know.

'Nothing at all to do with school,' Katie said firmly. With one hand she was dipping into her new shoulder bag, her fingers tightening round a bundle of envelopes.

She grinned at Lisa, who pulled one of her very funny faces. Then Lisa popped her fingers in and out of her ears to show it was time for the secret to be let out.

The two groups arrived at the same place at exactly the same moment. So between them they formed a large huddle. Vikki, noticing what was going on, raced towards them.

'Wait for me, wait for me!' she yelled. 'Don't do anything till I get there!'

Katie and Melanie waited until she joined them. With a quick look round, Vikki placed herself midway between Katie and Melanie.

'Go on, then,' she urged, folding her arms across her chest and rocking her head from side to side. 'I can see you've both got something special to say. So who's going first?'

'You can!' said Katie and Melanie in the same instant, each looking at the other and being very polite. It was such a surprise they'd both said exactly the same thing that everyone laughed.

'Oh well, me first then,' said Melanie with a smile. She quickly sorted through the pile of envelopes in her hand and gave one to Katie. 'Here you are, Katie, you get the first one.

It's an invitation to my birthday party the Sunday after next. I want everyone to be there. It's going to be very, very special.'

Katie stared. She couldn't believe what was happening.

'But, but . . .' She began again. 'But, Melanie, it's MY birthday party the Sunday after next. I've got an invitation here for you—and, well, everyone.'

'Oh no!' groaned Lisa. 'Not on the same day!'

'Hey, that's no good!' Simon said, looking very upset. 'If they're at the same time we'll have to miss out on one of them. I'd hate that!'

'Are they at the same time, Katie?' Jessica asked.

'Mine's in the afternoon,' Katie said, and glanced at Melanie. 'Is yours?'

Melanie just nodded.

'Well, you can change the day—one of you,' Vikki pointed out. 'Then everything will be fine. We can all go to two parties. Terrific!'

'I'd like that!' said Simon.

'Is Sunday your actual birthday, Katie?' Melanie wanted to know.

'Well, no, it's Saturday. But we have to go to London for my cousin's birthday on the Saturday. It's our turn to go there this year, Mum says. That's why we're having my party the next day. And Mum's getting some videos in London specially for my party.'

Melanie looked pleased with herself. 'We're having a real magician!' she said proudly. 'He's called Marvo the Magician. It's going to be a magic party.'

'Oh, that's terrific!' Vikki exclaimed.

'Wow!' said Simon, opening his eyes as wide as his mouth.

'Fantastic!' said Belinda.

'I've always wanted to see a real magician!' said Lisa.

'So have I,' said Vikki.

Katie said nothing, nothing at all. Her heart sank. I'd have liked to have a real magician at my party, too, she thought, but she knew that was impossible. All Mum's money seemed to go on their old car, the Moving Museum. Still, Mum was a brilliant cook, so the food would be special. And she was always full of ideas, so she'd be able to invent some good games. And then they'd have the videos.

My party will be magic in a different way, Katie told herself. She gave out her party invitations to everyone: and everyone looked pleased to get one. 'I'd like to come to both parties,' Simon announced.

'You're just greedy,' laughed Jessica.

Katie wondered which of her friends would come to her party. She particularly wanted Lisa to be there.

'You will come to my party, won't you?' she asked Lisa on their way back into school.

Lisa glanced across at Melanie. 'I don't know yet for sure, Katie,' she replied. 'Are you going to have a magician, too?'

'Maybe,' Katie said vaguely.

'Or maybe something even better.' Then, before Lisa could ask her any more questions, she ran inside.

After school Katie rushed straight home. Her mum was working on the car, which was parked outside the shed at the end of the lane. She was looking a bit fed up.

'Something wrong with the petrol pump,' she explained, jabbing at the engine. 'That's the trouble with old cars, there's always something to put right. Still, I'll get there in the end. Had a good day, darling?'

'Not really,' Katie replied, crossing her arms under her chin and looking very glum. Then she told her mum about the party problems. 'What can we do, Mum?'

'Well, there's one thing we could do, Katie,' her mum said. 'We could simply have your party on another day—perhaps the following week. Then—'

'Oh no!' Katie wailed. 'I'd

hate that! I mean, I wanted it on my proper birthday, on the Saturday. But I had to change it because of going to London. So I want the party as near as possible to the real day. I don't think birthdays should be moved about like, like the hands of a clock!'

Her mum laughed. 'Well, I

agree with you really,' she said. 'I just thought a change of date would give you a chance to go to Melanie's party.'

'I expect Melanie's will be good,' Katie admitted. 'But mine will be better.'

'You know what you are, don't you?' her mum said.

'What?' said Katie.

'You're stubborn, that's what!' said her mum. 'That's how you get your own way.'

Katie laughed. 'Could you make us some of that spooky food, Mum?' she asked. 'Cobweb squash and broomstick-burgers and those witch biscuits with red and green eyes? They're terrific!'

'Maybe,' said her mum. 'And we'll need something really special for the games. Actually, I was talking to Mrs Cheng down the lane today and she's given me rather a bright idea. Listen . . .'

At school next day Katie asked Lisa if she was coming to her party.

'Well . . .' Lisa began.

'You'll be missing something really good if you don't come,' Katie told her.

Lisa rolled her eyes, one of her favourite tricks. 'Such as?' she wanted to know.

'Well, listen to this: we're going to have a dragon at my party! A real, moving dragon with fire shooting out of its mouth! How about that?'

For once Lisa didn't make one of her funny faces. She just looked amazed.

'Will it really breathe out fire

that can, well, scorch you?' she asked.

'Of course. That's what proper dragons do, isn't it?' Katie replied.

'Why are you having a dragon at your party?' asked Vikki, who had just joined them and heard what Katie said.

'Because this year the Chinese New Year falls on my party day, that's why. And Chinese dragons always turn up at parties to celebrate the New Year. That's what Mrs Cheng says. And she's Chinese, so she should know. So that's how we're getting one. A proper Chinese dragon.'

'This I've got to see!' Lisa exclaimed.

'Me, too,' said Vikki.

'And me!' Simon chimed in. He had heard Lisa's excited voice and he, Jessica, Ross, Belinda and Sharmilla had all come to listen.

Katie was delighted. Mum's

great idea was working. Everyone wanted to be at her party.

'Well, you'll all have to wear something red,' she told them. 'That's very important.'

Lisa looked puzzled. 'Why, Katie?' she asked.

'Because that's the magic

colour for dragons,' said Katie. 'Didn't you know? The Chinese think red's a very lucky colour.'

'Will a red headband do?' Jessica asked.

'Well, if you like,' said Katie. 'But red tights will be better. People might not be able to see the headband.'

That puzzled everyone. 'Why?' they all wanted to know.

Katie grinned. 'You'll find out at the party. But you'll have to wait till then.'

'I wish your party was tomorrow, Katie,' Ross said with a sigh. 'I can't wait for it to begin. It'll be magic with a dragon.'

A few days later, at going home time, Melanie came to talk to Katie in the cloakroom.

'You know, Katie, you could still come to my party if you wanted to,' she said. 'I wish you would. You could easily just change the date of your party. Then I could come as well.'

'It can't be changed, Mel,' Katie replied. 'It's the Chinese New Year's Day. We're going to have some very special games. And the dragon's coming, of course. Why don't you change the date of your party? Then you could come to mine.'

Melanie shook her head and her long blonde hair danced. 'Marvo the Magician has been booked for ages. He's very popular, you know. He wouldn't be free on another day for—for months.'

'Oh well, I hope you have a great time,' Katie said cheerfully. 'I'm sure you will.'

'How many are going to your

party, Katie?' Melanie asked.

'Don't know exactly. But lots and lots, I think.'

'I thought so,' Melanie said.

'Hey, look at that!' Ross said excitedly to Belinda as they arrived at Katie's for the party. 'Look at that dragon's head on the door!'

'Shows we're at the right house,' Belinda said. 'I think this is going to be really good.'

It was such a cold winter's day that everyone was given a hot drink as they came in: a steaming mug of red fruit juice. 'It's what dragons drink to set their breath on fire!' Katie explained.

'Where's the real dragon, Katie?' Lisa wanted to know.

'He'll be here in a little while,' said Katie's mum. 'But first you've all got to look for him. I'd start in the old laundry room if I were you . . .'

Lisa was the first to get there because she knew Katie's house

so well. And there, lying on the washing machine, was a long green tail.

'Who made that?' Sharmilla wanted to know. 'It looks just like the real thing with those bubbly bits.'

'I helped Mum,' Katie said. 'She used some old felt.'

'It's got a message on,' Belinda said. She read aloud:

> 'To find the very next bit of me,
> Look closely where we keep the tea.

'What does that mean?' asked Ross.

'It's a clue in a treasure hunt,' explained Vikki. She had won a treasure hunt at another party. 'Where do you keep the tea, Katie?'

'You'll have to work that out,' Katie said.

'Must be the kitchen!' Ross said and so everyone rushed there. But it turned out to be the pantry and it was Sharmilla who found the next part of the dragon on a shelf near the teabags.

'Hey, you can fit it over your head,' Sharmilla said, lifting the green-painted hollow box to show everyone. 'And the tail fits this end. Oh, and there's another message . . .'

They had a hectic time hunting the missing pieces of the dragon's body all over the house and then fitting them together. The clues led them to the bathroom, the dining-room, then up to the attic and down to the cellar. At last the only part of the red-and-green-and-gold dragon left to find was its head.

Ross read out the final clue:

> 'If you look out of Katie's window,
> What you'll see is a dazzling glow.'

They all rushed upstairs to Katie's bedroom and crowded round the window, staring into the gloomy winter afternoon. Suddenly, a sparkler flared up—

then another—and yet another.
'Look!' Lisa yelled. 'A dragon's head, all lit up in the dark. Coming down the path on its own! That's magic!'

They all crowded closer, trying to get a better view.

'Look at the red fire in its mouth!' cried Ross.

It was a dazzling mask. Katie and her mum had painted it with luminous paint so that it glowed in the dark. Katie's mum was dressed in black, so no one could see her walking down the path, holding the mask up high.

She called to them: 'Come on down and change into a dragon!'

'Can we really all get into it?' Belinda asked when they were all in the sitting-room.

Katie's mum was busily making sure the body parts were all joined together.

'That's the idea,' she said. 'It's made so you can hold it on your shoulders. Only your legs will

show underneath. That's why
we wanted you to wear red
tights or red socks. This is the
amazing red-legged dragon!'

Katie and Lisa shared the big mask that was the head. They could each see out through an eye-hole. Lisa kept popping her tongue out through the mouth. Their friends lined up to make the body. The tail bounced along behind them.

'It's just like dressing up—only better,' Simon said.

'Come on, keep following me!' Katie called.

'Where are we going?' Ross asked. He was at the end.

'Visiting,' said Katie. 'First we're going to call on the Chinese family down the lane and wish them luck for the New Year. That's what dragons do on New Year's Day in China.'

'Oh, great!' said Sharmilla. 'We're going outside, just like a real parade. Everybody'll see us.'

Light snow was falling as the Great Red-Legged Dragon made its way slowly down the lane. Katie's mum kept setting

off fire-crackers. People out for a Sunday walk cheered and clapped when they met the amazing glowing dragon.

'We turn right here!' Katie yelled. And the red-legged dragon turned, a little awkwardly, into a wide gateway. Standing at the door were Mr and Mrs Cheng, clapping for joy. Mrs Cheng was wearing a red dress and her husband had on a red tie.

'Oh, thank you, thank you for coming,' they greeted the dragon. 'This is the best dragon visit we have ever had.'

'Happy New Year!' called out Katie and Lisa and their friends.

Mr Cheng handed an envelope to each of his visitors.

'It contains a present for you,'

he explained. 'It is a little money. One of our Chinese customs, you see. Happy New Year! Happy birthday, Katie!'

The dragon bowed and backed out of the gateway.

'Now where to?' asked Ross, when they were all in the lane.

'Wait and see,' said Katie mysteriously. She led the dragon round the corner and down the road. 'Stop!' she said.

They were outside Melanie's house.

Katie and Lisa peered through the eye-holes in the dragon's head. They could see Melanie and her friends in the front room, laughing at someone in a strange and marvellous costume. 'That must be Marvo the Magician,' whispered Lisa.

The dragon made its way up the path and Katie rang the doorbell. Melanie opened the door, looking very surprised.

'Happy Chinese New Year!'

Katie cried. 'Happy birthday, Melanie.' She and Lisa took off the dragon mask.

'Katie! Lisa! What a lovely surprise,' said Melanie. 'Come in, all of you, and meet Marvo the Magician.'

'Two parties in one day!' exclaimed Simon, who could hardly believe his luck.

'Two magic parties, you mean,' said Lisa and everyone laughed.